THE STRANGE CASE OF DR JEKYLL AND MR HYDE

BY ROBERT L. STEVENSON　　　RETOLD BY CARL BOWEN

ILLUSTRATED BY DANIEL PEREZ

COLOUR BY DANIEL PEREZ AND SEBASTIAN FACIO / PROTOBUNKER STUDIO

LIBRARIAN REVIEWER
Katharine Kan
Graphic novel reviewer and Library Consultant

READING CONSULTANT
Elizabeth Stedem
Educator/Consultant

www.raintreepublishers.co.uk
Visit our website to find out
more information about
Raintree books.

To order:
☎ Phone +44 (0) 1865 888066
🖷 Fax +44 (0) 1865 314091
💻 Visit www.raintreepublishers.co.uk

Raintree is an imprint of Capstone Global Library Limited, a company incorporated in
England and Wales having its registered office at 7 Pilgrim Street, London, EC4V 6LB –
Registered company number: 6695582

"Raintree" is a registered trademark of Pearson Education Limited, under licence to
Capstone Global Library Limited

Text © Stone Arch Books, 2009
First published by Stone Arch Books in 2009
First published in hardback in the United Kingdom in 2009
First published in paperback in the United Kingdom in 2010
The moral rights of the proprietor have been asserted.

Art Director: Heather Kindseth
Graphic Designer: Kay Fraser
Edited in the UK by Laura Knowles
Printed and bound in China by Leo Paper Products Ltd

ISBN 978-1406212570 (hardback)
13 12 11 10 09
10 9 8 7 6 5 4 3 2 1

ISBN 978-1406213591 (paperback)
14 13 12 11 10
10 9 8 7 6 5 4 3 2

British Library Cataloguing in Publication Data
Bowen, Carl.
The strange case of Dr. Jekyll and Mr. Hyde. -- (Graphic revolve)
741.5-dc22
A full catalogue record for this book is available from the British Library.

YA
1-- 4923

TABLE OF CONTENTS

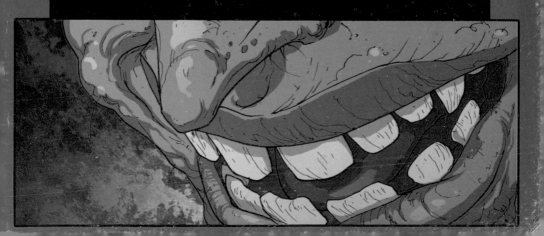

INTRODUCING . . .

POOLE,
THE BUTLER

GABRIEL UTTERSON

DR HENRY JEKYLL

4

HASTIE LANYON

EDWARD HYDE

5

"It happened some months ago, late at night in the Soho neighbourhood."

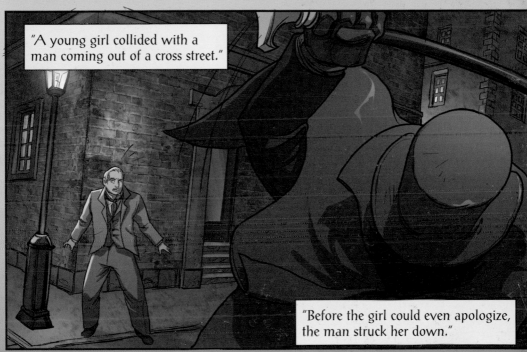

"A young girl collided with a man coming out of a cross street."

"Before the girl could even apologize, the man struck her down."

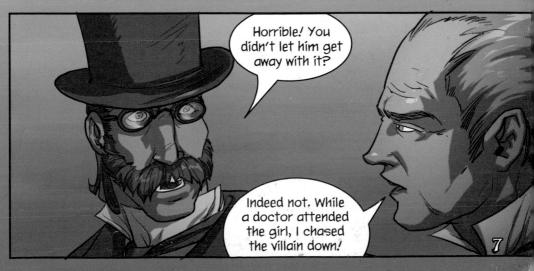

Horrible! You didn't let him get away with it?

Indeed not. While a doctor attended the girl, I chased the villain down!

7

The awful man then led us to this very property and to that rear door.

He returned with a portion of the sum in gold and wrote a cheque for the rest.

Did this brute have a key for that door?

Did he give you his name?

Yes. I don't believe he lives here, though.

His name was Edward Hyde.

Hyde? How strange.

9

I thought the man who lived here was Doctor Henry Jekyll.

That's right! His name was on the cheque to the poor girl's father. How did you know?

Jekyll owns this property and is a client of mine. I helped him prepare his will.

I see. If he's a client, we should speak no more of this.

Agreed. The less said the better. Now, please excuse me, Enfield.

CHAPTER 2

MEETING MR HYDE

Who are you?

My name is Utterson.

Utterson? Doctor Jekyll's attorney?

I'm also a friend of Henry Jekyll's. Do you mind if I come up?

You won't find Dr Jekyll here, sir. You should leave.

Very well.

But if I should meet you again, sir, how will I recognize you?

Ah, yes!

If that will be all, sir.

Yes, thank you, Poole.

Now, what causes you to worry, Utterson?

It's about that man in your will – Edward Hyde. I met him last night.

Is that so?

My cousin, Richard Enfield, has met him as well. He says Hyde came here for help after an incident in Soho.

Hyde has his own key to my laboratory in the back.

But why? Has he got some hold over you, Henry?

I fear that he means you harm.

19

21

A few months passed without word from Dr Jekyll or Mr Hyde. But then . . .

CHAPTER 4

OUT OF CONTROL

Who could be out so late at night?

Aargh!

SMACK

22

23

Do you know this man?

His name is Hastie Lanyon, an old friend. What happened to him, Inspector?

He was attacked on the street. A young lady who lives nearby saw the whole thing.

We found this lying in the gutter.

May I see that?

My God, I've seen this before!

I believe I know where the murderer lives!

25

Looks like he forgot to take his chequebook out of his pocket. You can't get far in this city without money.

If there's no money here, Hyde might try the bank.

Hyde won't try the bank, I'm sure of it.

There's someone else he can turn to for money.

A short time later . . .

Good morning, Poole. I must see Dr Jekyll.

Right this way, sir.

The Doctor's in his laboratory out the back. He's been there all night.

Henry! Are you ill?

No. I've had a terrible scare.

As have I, Henry. Our old friend Hastie Lanyon is dead.

He was murdered by Edward Hyde!

29

Weeks later, Jekyll's butler arrives at Utterson's house . . .

Poole! What brings you here? Is Henry ill?

Mister Utterson, there's something wrong. I've been afraid for about a week. I can bear it no more.

The Doctor has locked himself in his laboratory. I'm afraid for him, sir.

I think there's been foul play. Will you come with me and see for yourself?

Hyde has come back!! We must hurry!

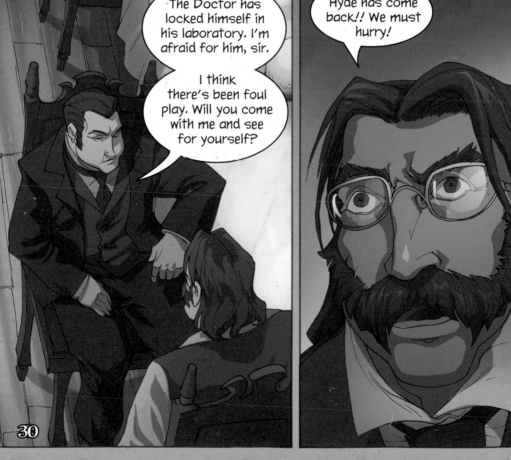

33

35

Utterson, I'm glad you're still here. We're almost finished inside.

Any sign of Henry Jekyll, Inspector?

I'm afraid not. His body's not in there. We'll dig up the yard, but I doubt we'll find anything.

We might never know what happened to Doctor Jekyll.

We found this envelope addressed to you. Since you're Jekyll's attorney, we can't open it before you look at it.

Thank you, Inspector.

What?

You don't confess unless you've done something wrong.

Henry Jekyll's Full Confession

Henry, what on earth could you have done?

37

"My name is Doctor Henry Jekyll. I was born in London to a wealthy family."

"My loving parents raised me in warmth and safety, wanting for nothing."

"Growing up, I think I enjoyed school more than my friends did."

CHAPTER 5

JEKYLL'S CONFESSION

"I studied hard, got good grades, and didn't waste much time playing."

"My hard work earned me a place at the best college in England."

"There I met Hastie Lanyon, who introduced me to Gabriel Utterson."

"The three of us became great friends."

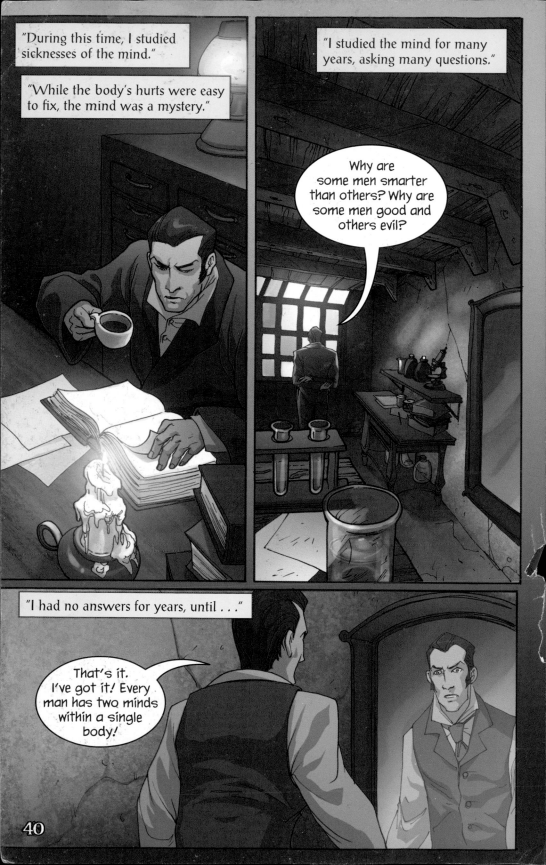

41

"In time, I explained this discovery to my friend Lanyon. Like me, he was a man of science. I hoped he might understand."

A neat idea, but not worth anything.

It's not like you can give those minds their own separate bodies.

"He didn't take me seriously."

Goodnight, Henry! From both of me! Ha ha ha!

"Lanyon was only joking, but what if I could separate the high and low minds from each other?"

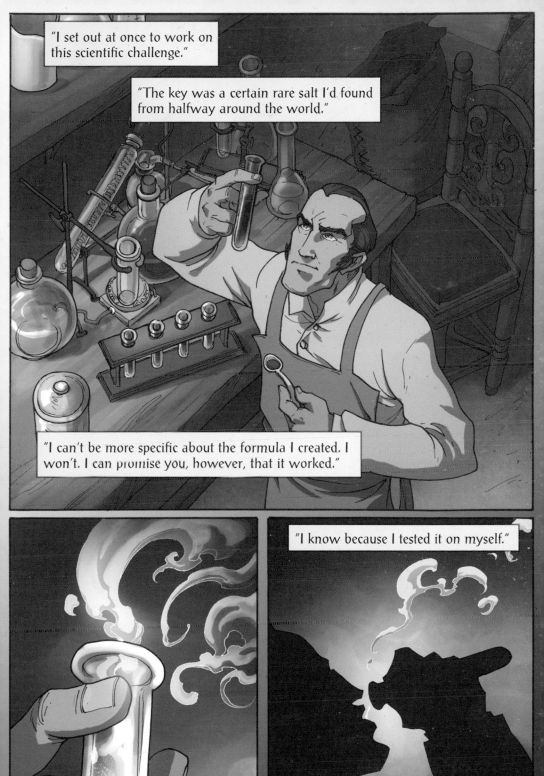

"I set out at once to work on this scientific challenge."

"The key was a certain rare salt I'd found from halfway around the world."

"I can't be more specific about the formula I created. I won't. I can promise you, however, that it worked."

"I know because I tested it on myself."

43

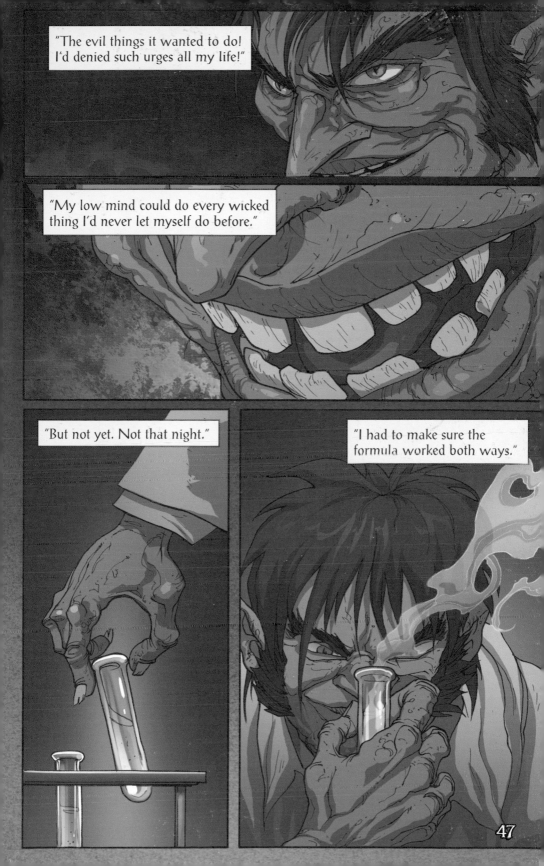

"The evil things it wanted to do! I'd denied such urges all my life!"

"My low mind could do every wicked thing I'd never let myself do before."

"But not yet. Not that night."

"I had to make sure the formula worked both ways."

"Lanyon made me leave at once. I'd never seen him so upset."

SLAM!

"Lanyon's reaction made me question everything I'd done."

Had I gone too far?

"That night, I decided to set aside my formula."

"I woke the next day. To my relief, my low mind was blessedly quiet."

"But then . . ."

SSSSSSSSS

What on earth?

"My body burned and twisted inside. I became Edward Hyde!"

SSSSSSSSSS

"Without my formula!"

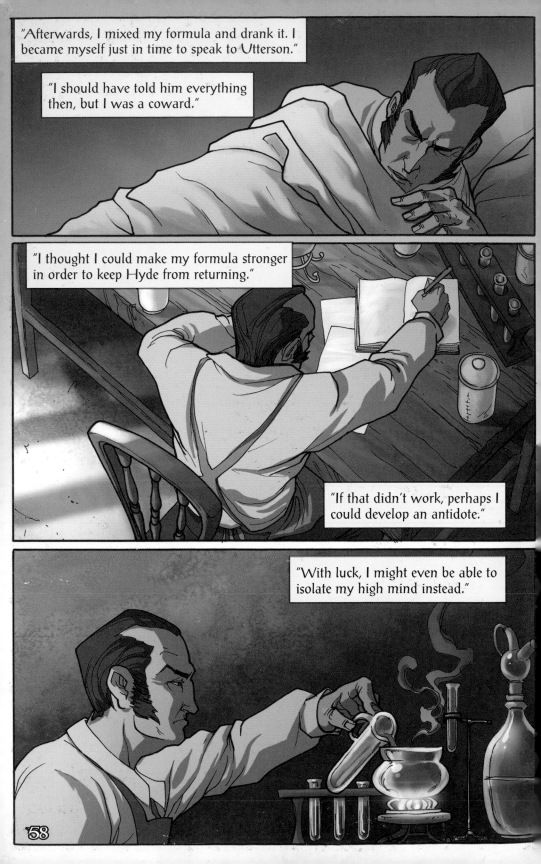

"Afterwards, I mixed my formula and drank it. I became myself just in time to speak to Utterson."

"I should have told him everything then, but I was a coward."

"I thought I could make my formula stronger in order to keep Hyde from returning."

"If that didn't work, perhaps I could develop an antidote."

"With luck, I might even be able to isolate my high mind instead."

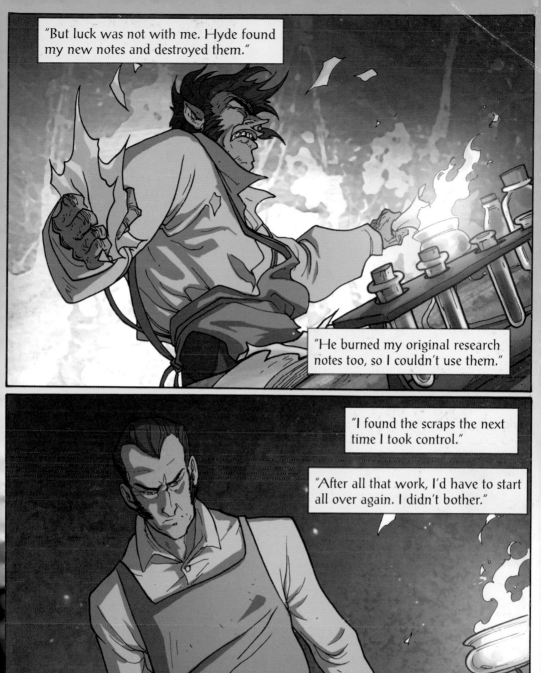

"But luck was not with me. Hyde found my new notes and destroyed them."

"He burned my original research notes too, so I couldn't use them."

"I found the scraps the next time I took control."

"After all that work, I'd have to start all over again. I didn't bother."

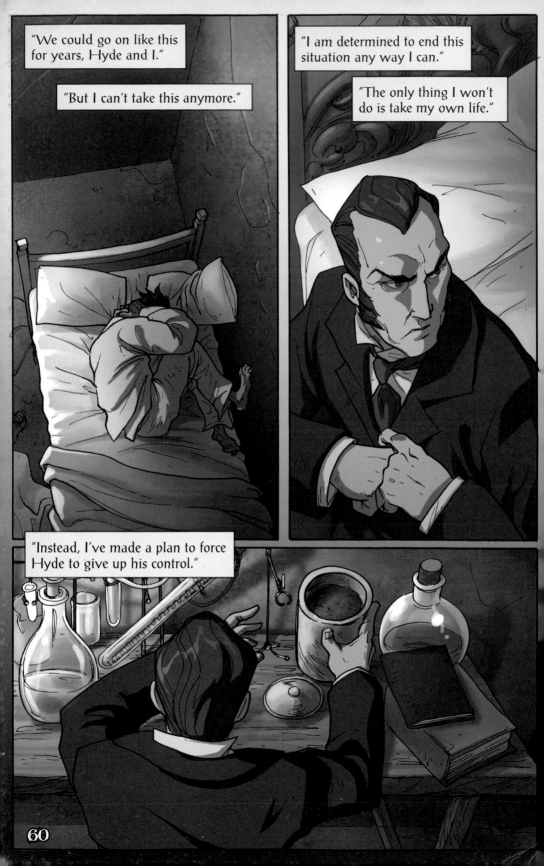

ABOUT THE AUTHOR

Robert Louis Stevenson was born in Scotland in 1850. His father, grandfather, and other ancestors were engineers, famous for the lighthouses they designed. Robert studied law for a while, then became a writer in his late twenties. He wrote articles about his travels in Europe and America, as well as such famous adventure stories as *Treasure Island* and *Kidnapped*. The original *Strange Case of Dr Jekyll and Mr Hyde* was published in 1886. Robert Louis Stevenson died eight years later.

ABOUT THE RETELLING AUTHOR

Carl Bowen is a writer and editor who lives in Georgia, USA. He was born in Louisiana, lived briefly in England, and was raised in Georgia, where he attended grammar school, high school, and college. He has published a handful of novels and more than a dozen short stories, all while working at White Wolf Publishing as an editor and advertising copywriter. His first graphic novel, published by Udon Entertainment, is called *Exalted*.

ABOUT THE ILLUSTRATOR

Daniel Perez was born in Monterrey, Mexico, in 1977. For more than a decade, Perez has worked as a colourist and an illustrator for comic book publishers such as Marvel, Image, and Dark Horse. He currently works for Protobunker Studio while also developing his first graphic novel.

GLOSSARY

antidote (AN-ti-dote) – something that stops a poison from working

attorney (ah-TUR-nee) – someone who draws up legal papers and helps people understand the law; an attorney is also called a "lawyer"

confession (kun-FEH-shun) – admitting you are guilty of doing something wrong

experiment (ek-SPER-uh-ment) – a controlled activity carried out to discover, test, or demonstrate something

formula (FOR-myuh-lah) – a recipe for how to make a substance; the substance made using that recipe is also called a formula.

inspector (in-SPEK-tur) – someone who checks or examines things; often called a detective

laboratory (LAB-rah-tor-ee) – a place equipped for making scientific experiments or tests

vain (VAYN) – being too proud of one's self

villain (VIL-uhn) – a wicked person

will (WIL) – a written document stating what should happen to someone's property and money when that person dies; "will" is short for "last will and testament"

A formula to separate the body's two minds is impossible, right? Well, don't be so sure. Many of the world's greatest medical advances seemed impossible when they were first discovered.

For hundreds of years, many people feared getting a virus called **smallpox**. This disease was impossible to cure and often deadly. In the late 1700s, a doctor in England named Edward Jenner noticed that farmers who worked near cattle never got the disease. He believed because the farmers had come in contact with another disease called cowpox, they had developed **immunity** (i-MYOO-nih-tee) to smallpox. In 1796, Jenner tested his theory. He put a small amount of cowpox into the arm of an eight-year-old boy. The **vaccine** (vak-SEEN) worked, and the boy never contracted smallpox.

Until the mid-1800s, surgeries to cure injuries or disease were extremely uncommon. Why? Before that, doctors didn't use **anaesthesia** (a-ness-THEE-zhuh) on their patients. Anaesthesia helps prevent pain during an operation. When scientist William T.G. Morton and others discovered anaesthetic chemicals, doctors and dentists could finally help their patients without hurting them.

MEDICAL DISCOVERIES

Some of the greatest medical discoveries have actually happened by accident. In 1895, scientist Wilhelm Roentgen was performing experiments on cathode rays (KATH-ode RAYZ). During the experiment, he noticed that these rays of electrons could "see through" solid objects. He called them **X-rays**. Today, X-rays are used to take pictures of bones, teeth, and organs.

Another famous accident happened in 1928. That year, Professor Alexander Fleming left a pile of Petri dishes in his laboratory sink. He noticed that mould growing on one of the dishes had killed a bacteria sample. After testing, Fleming discovered the mould was *Penicillium notatum.* Soon, other scientists would find that **penicillin** could be used to cure bacteria infections in humans.

Also during the 1920s, Frederick Banting and other doctors discovered **insulin** (IN-suh-lihn). This hormone helps regulate the level of sugar in the human body. By taking shots of insulin, people with a disease called **diabetes** (dye-ah-BEE-teez) could lead normal lives. Before the discovery, many diabetes patients died from the disease.

Before the 1950s, a disease called poliomyelitis, better known as polio (POH-lee-oh), infected thousands of children each year. The disease could cause paralysis and often led to death. In 1952, Dr Jonas Salk created a vaccine for the awful disease. Today, children continue to receive the vaccine and the disease has been nearly wiped out.

1. Should the lawyer Gabriel Utterson keep Dr Jekyll's confession a secret? Or, should he tell others what happened? Explain your answer.

2. Do you think Dr Jekyll was responsible for the evil things Mr Hyde did? Why or why not?

3. Each page of a graphic novel has several illustrations called panels. What is your favourite panel in this book? Describe what you like about the illustration and why it's your favourite.

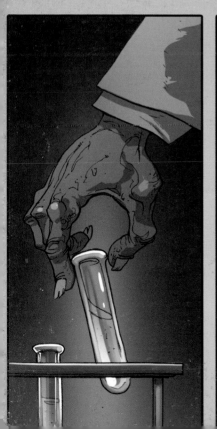

1. Dr Jekyll wrote about his frightening experience in a letter to Gabriel Utterson. Write a letter about your most frightening or exciting experience. Then, send the letter to a friend or family member.

2. At the end of the story, Gabriel Utterson finishes reading Dr Jekyll's confession. What do you think he'll do next? Will he tell the police? Will he keep the confession a secret? Write about it.

3. Dr Jekyll turned into a completely different person when he drank his formula. If you could be a completely different person, who would it be? Would you be a celebrity? The prime minister? Write about your experience as a different person.

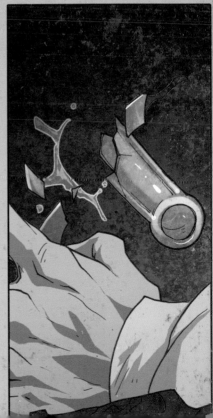

OTHER BOOKS

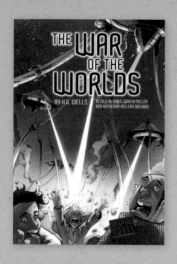

War of the Worlds

In the late 19th century, a cylinder crashes down near London. When George investigates, a Martian activates an evil machine and begins destroying everything in its path! George must find a way to survive a War of the Worlds.

The Hound of the Baskervilles

Late one night, Sir Charles Baskerville is attacked outside his castle in Dartmoor, Devon. Could it be the Hound of the Baskervilles, a legendary creature that haunts the nearby moor? Sherlock Holmes, the world's greatest detective, is on the case.

Dracula

On a business trip to Transylvania, Jonathan Harker stays at an eerie castle owned by a man named Count Dracula. When strange things start to happen, Harker investigates and finds the count sleeping in a coffin! Harker isn't safe, and when the count escapes to London, neither are his friends.

20,000 Leagues Under the Sea

Scientist Pierre Aronnax and his trusty servant set sail to hunt a sea monster. With help from Ned Land, the world's greatest harpooner, the men soon discover that the creature is really a high-tech submarine. To keep this secret from being revealed, the sub's leader, Captain Nemo, takes the men hostage. Now, each man must decide whether to trust Nemo or try to escape this underwater world.

GRAPHIC REVOLVE

If you have enjoyed this story, there are many more exciting tales for you to discover in the Graphic Revolve collection...

20,000 Leagues Under the Sea

Black Beauty

Dracula

Frankenstein

Gulliver's Travels

The Hound of the Baskervilles

The Hunchback of Notre Dame

King Arthur and the Knights of the Round Table

Robin Hood

The Strange Case of Dr Jekyll and Mr Hyde

Treasure Island

The War of the Worlds